Praise for Maureen Lee

'You'll be totally gripped by this wonderful tale'
Woman's Own

'With her talent for storytelling, queen of saga-
writing Maureen Lee weaves intrigue, love and
warmth into every page'   *My Weekly*

'Big on drama and there's enough excitement
packed into these pages to last a lifetime'
Now Magazine

Maureen Lee was born in Bootle, Merseyside, and now lives in Colchester, Essex. She is the author of several bestselling novels, and has also had numerous short stories published and a play staged. Her novel *Dancing in the Dark* won the 2000 Parker Romantic Novel of the Year Award. Visit her website at www.maureenlee.co.uk

By the same author

Amy's Diary

Maureen Lee

An Orion paperback

First published in Great Britain in 2012
by Orion Books Ltd,
Orion House, 5 Upper St Martin's Lane,
London WC2H 9EA

An Hachette UK company

1 3 5 7 9 10 8 6 4 2

A CIP catalogue record for this book
is available from the British Library.

ISBN 978 1 4091 3738 2

Typeset at The Spartan Press Ltd,
Lymington, Hants

Printed and bound in Great Britain by Clays Ltd,
St Ives plc

The Orion Publishing Group's policy is to use papers that
are natural, renewable and recyclable products and made
from wood grown in sustainable forests. The logging and
manufacturing processes are expected to conform to the
environmental regulations of the country of origin.

www.orionbooks.co.uk

For Fay and Fenella

Chapter One

My name is Amy Browning and today, 3 September 1939, is my eighteenth birthday. The day I decided to keep a diary.

A lot has happened already. At two o'clock this morning my sister Jean had her second baby, a boy this time. She's going to call him Mickey. And just a few hours later it was announced on the wireless that Great Britain had gone to war with Germany.

It's Sunday and I'd been to church with Mam and Dad so we didn't know about the war until we got home. Germany, led by the dictator Adolf Hitler, had invaded Poland, something that Britain had warned it not to do.

It's been a lovely sunny day. In Opal Street, Liverpool, where we live, everyone was standing outside, talking about the war. It wasn't a surprise as we'd been expecting it for months. A brick air-raid shelter had been built at the end of our street. Once the sirens went, we'd have to go there until we heard the all-clear.

Mam shuddered and said to Dad, 'Just

imagine, Joe, sitting in that shelter with bombs falling all around us.'

'Don't worry, Mary,' Dad said. 'It won't come to that.'

'Then why have the government built shelters in nearly every street in Liverpool?' Mam snapped. 'And why has our Harry had to join the army?' She burst into tears. 'Now he'll be sent away to fight. Oh, Joe, what if our Harry is killed?'

My older brother Harry is in an army camp not far away in Preston. I didn't want to think about him being killed.

We went indoors and had our dinner, although nobody spoke much. When we'd finished, I said, 'I'm going to see Sally. We might go for a walk.'

Sally Clarke is my best friend and she lives around the corner in Coral Street. We'd gone to the same school and been in the same class. Now we worked in the same place, in the steam room of Reed's Dye Factory. We both hated it. I mean, who wants to spend their whole life pressing other people's clothes? Well, I certainly don't and neither does Sally.

Sally's front door was open and her gran was sitting on the front step. Like those in Opal Street, the houses were terraced and didn't have front gardens. There was just a little yard with an outside toilet at the back.

'Sal's upstairs,' her gran said when she saw me, moving aside to let me in. The house was noisy. Very loud music was coming from the wireless and Sally's mam and dad were yelling at each other in the kitchen. They had fights all the time.

'Sal,' I called as I ran upstairs.

Sally came out of her room. She was very pretty with blonde hair and bright blue eyes. Her five older sisters were all married and had left home.

'Happy birthday,' she said. 'I've got you a present. Eh, what do you think about the war?' Without waiting for me to answer, she went on, 'Our Cora said there's really good jobs going at Gregg's, a factory in Speke where they make guns, bullets and tanks.'

I knew Britain was short of munitions. We were going to need a good deal more of them to fight a war with a well-equipped country like Germany. 'What sort of jobs?' I asked.

'All different sorts. They pay really good wages, at least three or four pounds a week.' She wrinkled her nose. 'The only bad thing about it is that it's shift work. They work from six in the morning until two in the afternoon one week, and the next week it's from two until ten o'clock at night.'

'I wouldn't mind that,' I said. 'Not for three or four pounds a week.' Our wages at Reed's were less than a pound each. 'Could we get jobs at this place?'

'Cora said all we've got to do is write them a letter and ask. She's got the address. We could write tonight.'

We climbed over Sal's gran to get out of the house. I told Sal about our Jean and the new baby. 'It's a boy and she's calling him Mickey. Shall we go to the maternity hospital to see them?'

'Okay.' Sal linked my arm in hers. 'You know, even though we're at war with Germany, everything's still exactly the same. The sun's still shining, the birds are still in the sky.' She looked at the seagulls flying above. 'Later on, night will come just as it always does. Nothing's changed.'

'Why does there have to be a war anyway? So many people are going to be killed. You'd think people could settle arguments in a better way.'

Sally shrugged her shoulders. 'My dad said it will all be over in six months, but Mam thinks it will take longer. It's what they were fighting about. Whatever happens, I think it's going to be exciting. Liverpool is one of the biggest ports in the world so there'll be loads of sailors around. The dances will be full of them.'

Well, that was something to look forward to. Sally and I went dancing two or three times a week.

At the hospital, our Jean looked happy, but tired. Jean was several years older than me and we looked very alike. We both had the same brown curly hair and darker-brown eyes. Mam describes us as nice looking rather than pretty. Jean's husband Dennis was away at sea and didn't know he'd become a father again. Mickey, the baby, was huge and looked more than just a few hours old.

'He weighed nine pounds three ounces,' Jean announced. 'He didn't half hurt.'

I was shocked and Sally gasped. I said, 'I bet he did.'

I doubted whether I could ever bring myself to have a baby. The very idea frightened me.

'Where's Emily?' Emily was Jean's daughter who was two.

'Mam's taken her back to the house for your birthday party. Many happy returns, by the way.' She pulled me towards her and kissed me on the cheek. 'There's a present for you at home. I'll give it to you another day.'

I was looking forward to my party. 'Mum's made a smashing cake. We'll save you a slice,' I promised. We were having ham, tomatoes and potato salad, followed by jelly and custard. 'Grandad's coming, Auntie Eileen, and Sally. And of course Mam and Dad and me.'

'What about our Alice?'

'She's on duty and can't get away.'

Our sister Alice was a staff nurse at Mossley Hill Hospital. We were all really proud of her. Training to be a nurse was really hard and took years, but Alice had earned top marks for everything.

Sal and I said goodbye to Jean and went for a walk along the Dock Road. It was very busy despite it being Sunday. Big ships were loading or unloading their cargoes. Horses pulled carts piled with crates of fruit or sacks of grain along the road, which was full of traffic. Dozens of different languages could be heard coming from the foreign seamen who pushed their way along the crowded pavements.

I sighed happily. The Dock Road was my favourite place. Apart from our house, I'd sooner be there than anywhere else in the world. I loved the smell of spices, exotic perfumes and foreign fruit. Above everything else I was aware of the salty tang of the River Mersey flowing nearby.

I really enjoyed my party. Mam and Dad had bought me a purse with a clasp and five pockets. They had put a penny in it for good luck, the good luck meaning it would never be empty. Grandad gave me a box of chocolates, Auntie Eileen a pretty georgette scarf and Sally a bottle of Evening in Paris scent. When Emily, my niece, sat on my knee I dabbed scent behind her tiny white ears.

I was feeling pretty happy with myself when our Harry turned up in his army uniform. He hadn't got me a present, but I was so pleased to see him I didn't care. I threw my arms around him and gave him a hug. Mam, who had been worrying about him all day, burst into tears. She made him sandwiches out of the ham that was left over and opened a tin of cream to go with the remainder of the jelly.

It had been a perfect party, but then it became even more perfect when the front door opened and Alice came in. My sister is the most beautiful person I have ever known. She has dark-green eyes and long hair the colour of autumn leaves, a sort of reddish gold. When I go out with our Alice, everyone turns their head to stare and it's not at me.

'Happy birthday, Sis,' she cried. 'I managed to persuade the hospital Matron to give me a few hours off, but I can't stay long.'

I was really pleased. It meant that all the family, apart from Jean, had managed to come to my birthday party. It made me feel very emotional. I loved them all so much.

'I haven't had time to buy you a present, Amy,' Alice said, 'but a patient gave me this the other day. I think he was from India.' She handed me a large book with a brown leather cover painted with gold flowers. 'It would be a shame to use it for my nursing notes and get it covered with stains, so I thought I'd give it to you.'

'Thank you.'

The book felt heavy in my hands, and the surface was as smooth as velvet. When I opened it the pages were cream with faint brown lines. It smelled too of strongly perfumed flowers that I didn't know the names of. It was one of the nicest presents I'd ever had. Alice also gave me a new pencil and a pencil sharpener.

'I remember when I lived at home I could never find a sharpener for my pencil,' she said.

'From now on, that notebook, pencil and sharpener must never be parted.'

My friend Sally stayed until it had gone dark so that we could go outside and see what it was like in the blackout. Every house in the country now had blackout curtains on the windows, so that not so much as a pinprick of light could be seen from the air.

With any luck, this would help to protect us from the German bombers that would be bound to target such a big port as Liverpool.

Outside, there was no moon and no stars. Sally and I could hardly see each other. I fell off the pavement because I couldn't see the kerb.

'I'm frightened,' I said.

'So am I.' Sally's voice shook.

Footsteps could be heard across the street. A man called out, 'Who's there?'

'It's Amy Browning and Sally Clarke,' I called back.

'Be careful where you go. It's not safe for young women to be out in the blackout.'

The man hadn't said who he was. I reached for Sally's hand. 'I think we'd better go home. I'll come to the corner with you.'

*

It was later that night that I decided to start writing a diary, in the notebook that an Indian patient had given to my lovely sister. I wrote what you have read so far, while sitting on the edge of my bed and resting the diary on the bedside table. Although I didn't promise myself that I would write in it every single day, I would try to write something at least once a week until the war is over.

I wondered how old I would be then. I said a little prayer that the war would end before I reached my next birthday.

Chapter Two

Two weeks later, Sally and I went for an interview at Gregg's Tool Company in Speke. We had to catch two buses to get there, but neither of us minded, just as we didn't mind the idea of working shifts. I minded less than Sally who found it hard to get up early.

At Reed's Dye Factory we were often accused of being lazy, but at Gregg's the manager, Mr Fuller, seemed very keen to have us. He told us we seemed to be a 'bright pair'.

Sally was given a job as an assistant in the stores where the workers went to get the bits and pieces to make engines for aeroplanes.

'You'll have to learn where everything is,' Mr Fuller told Sally, 'so you don't keep people waiting when they ask for a particular part.' There were shelves and shelves of tools, pieces of metal, and boxes of nuts and bolts. 'You'll need to remember where the sizes are too.'

He turned to me. 'As for you, young lady, we were very impressed with the letter you wrote to us. Very neat handwriting, I must say. So we thought we'd give you a job in the office. You'll be doing clerical work and dealing with supplies. I'll show you where your desk is.'

I was going to have a desk of my own. I could hardly believe it. The wages were agreed. We would earn two pounds, seventeen shillings and sixpence a week and be given a rise in the New Year if our work was up to standard.

Outside, we both wanted to rush home and tell our mams about our jobs. But we decided to celebrate by going into town and having a cup of tea in one of the posh teashops. Afterwards, I bought a lipstick and Sally bought a pair of pearl earrings in Woolworth's – where nothing cost more than sixpence.

Back home, I was thrilled to find our Harry there, but he'd only come to tell us that on Sunday he was being posted with the army to France. As expected, Mam was sick with worry.

'But it's what happens when there's a war on, Ma,' Harry told her patiently. 'France is where the fighting will be, so that's where men get sent. I don't want to be sitting around in some camp over here, twiddling my thumbs, instead of fighting.'

'Fighting!' Mam looked as if she was about to have a fit. 'Anyway, you're hardly a man yet.' She spoke as if Harry was still a little boy. Perhaps in her eyes he still was.

'I'm old enough to vote and get married – and fight for my country.' Harry patted Mam's arm. 'Don't worry, Ma. I'll come back safe and sound.'

Dad had just got in from work. He butted in. 'Don't be so cocky, lad. You look after yourself. Do you hear?'

'Yes, Dad,' Harry said meekly.

I didn't say anything, but I reckon inside our Harry was really frightened.

The streets of Liverpool had been strangely quiet for weeks. All the children had been sent to places like North Wales and Southport where they would be safe from the bombing when it started.

But by the time Christmas came and there'd been no sign of bombs anywhere, the children began to return home. The two little boys who lived next door walked all the way home from Southport along the railway tracks, much to the horror of their mother.

'You could have been killed,' she screamed. 'Here's me thinking you were safe when you could have been knocked down by a train.' She used an awful lot of swear words, but I'm not prepared to write them down in my diary.

It snowed heavily that winter. I loved it. Liverpool looked wonderful, particularly in the moonlight when the snow shone like silver. Mind you, it was no fun getting up at half past four when we were on the early shift and catching freezing-cold buses to the factory.

Sally and I really enjoyed working there. In the stores, Sally had quickly learned where everything was. It was my job to write out orders for supplies, anything from lavatory paper to pencils, and from overalls for the women working on the machines to light bulbs. Until the war started, all the machine workers had been men, but now that so many of them had been called up to fight, the women had taken over.

Our Harry wrote often. He was having a fine old time in France where he seemed to do nothing but drink wine. At least it meant he was safe. As I said before, there'd been no bombing. As far as the war went, nothing much was happening.

I said something to that effect at home one day and our Jean nearly bit my head off.

'You don't know what you're talking about,

you stupid girl,' she shouted. 'Hundreds of British merchant seamen have drowned when their ships were sunk by German torpedoes. My Dennis risks his life every single day to make sure food and other supplies get through. What would you do without your cuppa? You want to read the newspapers more often, girl. You haven't a clue what's going on.'

From then on, I bought the *Daily Mirror* every day from the newspaper seller outside Gregg's Tools. No one would say again I didn't know what was going on.

Everyone in the country had been given ration books full of coupons for everything from food to clothing. When you wanted to buy something the shopkeepers would cut out the coupon for it. We didn't have to use them until after Christmas 1939. From then on, we would no longer be able to buy whatever food we wanted, but would be limited to a small amount of nearly everything each week. For instance, we were only allowed four ounces of meat, four ounces of butter and twelve ounces of sugar.

The tea ration was two ounces each, which wasn't nearly enough. Though no one in our house complained when we thought about

Dennis risking his life to fetch it from India and other faraway places.

It was funny, really. Our family had always been hard up. Dad worked on the docks where the pay was low. Now all the young men there had been called up and were in the services – the army, navy or air force. In order not to lose the older men like my dad to factories where they could earn twice as much, the dock bosses had to increase their wages. What with me giving Mam half my wages for my keep and the army sending home Harry's pay, all of a sudden our family was well off.

But there was nothing much to spend the money on. Due to rationing, Mam was buying less food than before the war. One good thing was that she started buying butter as well as margarine. We couldn't afford butter before. There weren't as many clothes in the shops nowadays, nor much in the way of make-up.

I ended up starting a Post Office account, though I would far sooner have spent every penny of my wages rather than save them.

So far, I haven't said anything in my diary about a boyfriend. It's not because I haven't got one because I have. Well, a sort of boyfriend. I'm not the least bit serious about him.

His name is Ian Taylor. I met him through our Harry, back when they used to play football together. Sometimes on Saturdays all four of us would go dancing at the Locarno ballroom together – me and Sally, Ian and Harry. Ian is tall and quite handsome, but there's no way I shall marry him, no matter how many times he asks. He proposes at least once a month.

Now Ian has finished his training to be a motor mechanic and is about to join the Royal Air Force. He wants us to get engaged. I didn't like turning him down flat and promised to think about it.

'Tell him no,' Mam said sternly. 'You're much too young.'

'She's eighteen,' our Jean said.

She was round at our house all the time while Dennis was away. By now, Mickey was eight months old and a noisy, active baby. He was sitting on her knee, sucking a dummy and banging the table with a rattle. He smiled a lot and made happy gurgling noises, while his older sister Emily played underneath the table with her doll.

'I was engaged at seventeen and married at nineteen,' Jean said. 'It hasn't done me any harm.'

'Yes, but you were in love with Dennis.' Mam

made a face. She didn't like Dennis all that much, though she had never told Jean this. 'Our Amy isn't in love with Ian, is she?'

'Only Amy knows that.' Jean made a different sort of face. I have no idea what it meant.

Anyway, at the beginning of May, Ian went away to join the air force with my photo in his wallet, but I had still refused to get engaged.

According to the *Daily Mirror*, since the fighting had started, Britain wasn't doing all that well. With Adolf Hitler in charge, Germany was taking over more and more countries in Europe. When the German army invaded France, there was actually talk of the British being beaten, even of actually *losing* the war.

There was a huge fuss in the House of Commons. The Prime Minister, Neville Chamberlain, thought by most people to be too tired and too old for the job, was replaced by Winston Churchill – who was well liked and very capable. The entire country breathed a sigh of relief. Good old Churchill would never let us lose.

The German army was slowly fighting its way through France. British and French soldiers were being driven back towards the port of

Dunkirk where, trapped, they waited on the beaches for the boats to bring them back to Britain.

I shall never forget the day in June when Sal and I watched the news in the cinema and saw the hundreds of boats sailing across the English Channel to rescue the soldiers from Dunkirk. There were big boats and little boats, sailing boats and motor boats. The *Royal Daffodil*, the ferry boat on which Sal and I had sailed across the Mersey loads of times, was part of the fleet. I'm not ashamed to say that we both cried our eyes out.

Of course, Mam was in a terrible state, convinced our Harry must have been killed in the fighting. Mind you, we were all worried. Although we kept our fears to ourselves, not wanting to make Mam feel worse.

I was on an early shift at Gregg's Tools when the telephone rang at about eleven o'clock.

'It's for you, Amy,' called Frances James who was in charge of the office. She gave me the phone.

'Amy.' It was our Jean. She was calling from a telephone box. 'A letter's come from Harry. He's safe and sound in Dover and hopes to come home on leave soon.'

'Thank goodness,' I shouted.

Everyone in the office knew that Harry was in France and must have realised what had happened. They came and patted my shoulders, shook my hand and kissed me. They were almost as pleased as I was.

It was a wonderful feeling to know that almost every serviceman had been saved. In the House of Commons, Winston Churchill made a really brilliant speech. I listened to it on the wireless with Mam and Dad that same night.

'We shall defend our island home,' he said in his deep, gruff voice. 'We shall fight in France, we shall fight on the seas and oceans, we shall fight in the air. We shall never surrender.'

'And so say all of us,' Dad shouted as he punched the air.

Harry came home a few days later. His feet were covered in blisters. Somehow or other, he'd managed to lose his socks on the march to Dunkirk and his army boots were falling to pieces.

It happened that my boyfriend Ian had a few days' leave at the same time. I had to admit he looked extremely smart in his blue-grey uniform. He'd been stationed in Scotland and so far hadn't left the safety of the British Isles.

On Saturday, all four of us (Harry's blistered feet forgotten) went dancing at the Locarno ballroom. Mam wasn't very pleased. She liked Sally well enough, but didn't consider her good enough for Harry. She would have liked her only son to marry one of the royal princesses, Elizabeth or Margaret.

Anyway, we had a fine old time between us. I let Ian kiss me three times. He took ages with the last one and I was a bit sorry when he stopped.

Next morning, he came round to say goodbye and I was a bit sorry again when he left. We had no idea when we would next see each other.

I didn't exactly cry, but I felt quite sad when I wrote in my diary before I went to bed. A few days later, a letter arrived from Ian to say he had been sent to Egypt.

Chapter Three

At the end of June 1940, for the first time the air-raid siren went in Liverpool. It was after midnight and most people were fast asleep, including me. I woke up wondering what the horrible noise was, the loud up-and-down wail. It was like a large animal in pain. After a few terrifying minutes, I realised it was the siren.

Mam opened the bedroom door. 'Are you all right in there, girls?' she asked.

'Yes, Mam,' I said in a low voice. 'Alice hasn't woken up.'

My sister was in bed with me. Every now and then she spent a night at home. She worked so hard in the hospital and was so tired that she usually fell asleep the second her head touched the pillow.

I lay completely still beside her, listening to her steady breathing. I thought how much I loved both my sisters, as well as our Harry who had been posted to India, where tea came from. And Mam and Dad, of course. I prayed hard that nothing bad would happen to any of them.

The siren stopped and I lay waiting for the sound of German aeroplanes, laden with bombs to drop on us. But nothing happened. After a while, there was another sound. It was the siren again, but this time it was the all-clear. The air-raid warning must have been a false alarm. Alice still didn't wake up and was amazed next morning when I told her the siren had gone off.

'You didn't miss anything,' I told her.

There were more false alarms in July, but in August bombs were dropped across the River Mersey in Birkenhead and this time a young woman was killed. Over the next few weeks the siren went off quite a few times. Bombs fell, but always in fields outside the city.

So far, Mam had refused to go to the shelter or even get out of bed when the siren sounded. Dad went downstairs a few times while the raids were happening and made us cups of tea.

All the time the number of raids were increasing and getting closer and closer to home. I felt helpless. Everybody did. It was scary, knowing that more and more planes were coming and that the time would come when they would drop more bombs. Two had been dropped on ships very close to our home.

One night the siren went and round the

edges of the blackout curtains I could see that the sky had turned bright green. It was the brilliant light of a hundred incendiary bombs, made to cause fires, being dropped not far away from where we lived.

In September, when my birthday came round again, I refused to have a party. I just wasn't in the mood for celebrating.

These days, when the siren went, we had started going to the air-raid shelter at the end of the street. But some people had begun to sleep there early in the evening, whether or not the siren had gone. It was so crowded that there were often no seats left and you had to sleep on blankets on the floor. After the pubs closed, crowds of men would turn up having drunk too much. They sang their heads off and peed out of the door. The shelter stank. I didn't sleep a wink and neither did Mam. (Dad had become a fire-watcher and spent his nights lying on roofs down by the docks, ready to put out fires from the incendiary bombs.)

I told Mam I wasn't prepared to spend one more night in the shelter. I also told her I'd heard that some people stayed in their cupboards under the stairs during the raids.

'There'd be room enough in ours for the two of us,' I said.

Mam nodded in agreement. 'There would an' all. Let's sort the cupboard out now.'

I was on the late shift that week so I could help her. We dragged everything out of the cupboard under the stairs. The mops and brooms, the feather duster, the clothes horse, tins of this and bottles of that, a bundle of old clothes waiting for the rag-and-bone man.

When the cupboard was completely empty it looked quite big. The cobwebs were brushed away (with the feather duster) and the walls sponged down.

'What shall we sit on?' Mam asked. 'We'd never fall asleep on hard kitchen chairs. And there's no way I'd move the armchairs from the three-piece suite in the parlour. Anyway, they're far too big.'

'We could use the easy chairs from the living room,' I suggested. 'It wouldn't take a minute to carry them in when the siren goes and bring them out again the next day.'

The chairs had padded backs and seats and wooden arms. With a couple of pillows, I was sure I'd manage to sleep quite comfortably.

'That's a good idea.' Mam looked thoughtful. 'You know, I wouldn't mind buying a couple of new chairs for the living room. Me and your dad can go to town on Saturday and take a look around the shops. I'm sure there'll still be furniture for sale, if not much else. It'll be nice to spend our money on something really useful.'

I'd heard people say before, 'It was like hell on earth.' They might be talking about a rowdy football match, a thunderstorm, or a shop with a sale on and crowds fighting to be served. But nowadays, life really was like hell on earth. It didn't happen every night, but most evenings the siren would go at around seven o'clock, maybe, or at midnight, or in the early hours of the morning. Some nights it would go twice.

The siren would be followed by the menacing growl of enemy planes, the Heinkels, Junkers and Dorniers, on their way to Liverpool with their deadly load of bombs.

The air-raid shelter at the end of the street next to ours was hit by a bomb. People I'd known all my life were killed, including a girl I'd gone to school with.

Going into work, I'd find that the woman who brought round the tea trolley was no longer there, or the old man who cleaned the lavatories. Either they'd died when their street had been bombed the night before or they were in hospital, badly injured. People were being killed in their hundreds. It was like a nightmare, except that we were all wide awake and it was really happening.

Buildings were disappearing too: famous shops, theatres, public houses and hospitals. Landmarks that had stood for centuries were reduced to rubble overnight.

And what was truly amazing was that some nights, in the middle of the worst of the bombing, the people in the air-raid shelter in our street could be heard singing.

'There's a long, long trail a'winding,' they sang, or 'Pack up your troubles in your old kitbag and smile, smile, smile.'

They refused to let Adolf Hitler get them down. The British people would never give up or give in.

Christmas week was the worst yet. On 20 December 1940, 50 German planes bombed the city for nine and a half hours without stopping. The next night was much worse when 150 planes attacked and the raid continued from half past seven in the evening until a quarter past five next morning. There was no let-up, not even on Christmas Eve. On

Christmas morning, I went into the parlour to find an explosion had caused all the soot to fall down the chimney. Our Christmas tree and the decorations were completely black.

Jean's husband, Dennis, was home for Christmas. They came to dinner with their kids. From India, Harry wrote to say that there wasn't much in the way of fighting going on there, at least not yet. Auntie Eileen had returned to Ireland, which was where Mam's family came from. Grandad lived over a butcher's shop in Marsh Lane and had come to every Christmas dinner at our house since before I was born. It would have felt peculiar without him. As you can imagine, we hardly saw anything of our Alice these days as the hospital was always busy.

Anyway, we all pretended to be cheerful. After a while, we really did feel cheerful. We were all still alive and our house was still standing, and we had enough to eat. Both Mam and Jean had each managed to buy a chicken for the dinner. The children, Emily and Mickey, made us laugh.

Despite the shortage of things in the shops, we'd all managed to buy each other presents. Mam knitted non-stop while we sat under the stairs during the bombing. She'd made cardigans for us women, including Emily, and pullovers for the men. Mickey was presented with a very attractive knitted teddy bear wearing a blue and white striped Everton football scarf.

On New Year's Eve, Alice came to tea. She looked very thin and pale, yet more beautiful than ever. As beautiful as a saint, Mam said after she'd gone.

Of course we sang 'Auld Lang Syne'. There wasn't a raid that night so we went outside and sang it again while holding hands with our neighbours.

> *Should auld acquaintance be forgot*
> *And never brought to mind*
> *Should auld acquaintance be forgot*
> *And days of old lang syne.*

At midnight, we listened to the chimes of Big Ben on the wireless, announcing that it was 1941.

Every now and then we'd think the raids were slowing down, or becoming fewer. Then there'd be one lasting all night long, and the attack was so heavy and destructive that we'd wonder whether we'd live the whole night through. I imagined that, by the time the raid ended, there'd be no part of Liverpool left standing or anyone left alive.

It continued like that for month after month, until the second day of May when that night all hell broke loose, this time with a vengeance.

I don't have the words to describe it. Mam and I clung to each other as our house shook and the bricks groaned. We could hear screams outside. A dog kept barking. Mam wanted to go and fetch it in, but I wouldn't let her.

'Let's hope your dad's all right,' she kept saying.

Our Jean and the kids had gone to spend the night with Dennis's mother in Maghull where the raids hardly ever reached.

A bomb fell and glass shattered. Somewhere in the house a window had broken. I thought I could hear bricks, or perhaps it was slates, dropping into our backyard. It was impossible to sleep, impossible to think.

At long last morning came. Directly opposite our house there was a pile of rubble where two houses had once stood. Fortunately, no one had been killed, as the people who lived there had been in the shelter. The only damage we had was some bricks that had fallen off the wall in the backyard and a broken kitchen window.

We were so relieved when Dad came home. 'I don't think I'll ever sleep again after what I saw last night,' he muttered. 'It's not right, it can't be right, that people should suffer like that. It's sheer, bloody savagery.'

There was a knock on the door. I opened it to a woman I'd never seen before. Her clothes and her hair were thick with dust. She introduced herself as a nurse from Mossley Hill Hospital. She had come to tell us that last night the hospital had been hit by a high-explosive bomb and our Alice had been killed.

Chapter Four

For a long while, nothing mattered. Mam still managed to keep the house clean, Dad went to work during the day and fire-watched at night. I went to and from Gregg's. I never missed a single shift, though sometimes I was late because the raids had lasted for so long. There were nights when we had to sleep in the factory basement because there would be an air raid and it wasn't safe to leave until it ended.

In fact, at Gregg's I was promoted. I was moved from the office and shown how to work a drilling press that turned out little metal parts for aeroplanes. I had to wear navy-blue overalls and hide my hair under a scarf tied like a turban. My weekly wages went up to four pounds, two shillings and sixpence. But I didn't really care. I didn't care about anything, now that my sister was dead.

'I wish it had been me,' I said to Sally. 'Our Alice was so much more useful as a human being than I am. I mean, she helped people get better and saved their lives. And she was so sweet and I'm so horrible.'

'Oh, Amy, don't talk so daft,' Sally would say or something like that. She was really upset about Alice too. Everybody in the street was. You wouldn't believe the number of people who came to her funeral and the amount of flowers that they sent.

Ian wrote a really lovely letter from Egypt where he was stationed. He said he remembered Alice from school. She was two years older than he was.

'One day I fell over in the playground and badly cut my knee. She helped me indoors and bathed the cut until someone came and bandaged it.' This was long before Alice had become a nurse.

Over the next months, between our Alice dying and Christmas 1941, there were very few air raids. In November they stopped altogether. I'd had another birthday and was now twenty. I still wrote in my diary at least once a week and every time the lovely, delicate scent from the pages reminded me of my lost sister.

Food was scarce at Christmas, and presents even scarcer, but somehow we managed to put on a good show. To my surprise, Ian came home on a week's leave. He looked very brown and very attractive. When he first turned up at our house, I wanted to throw my arms around his neck and he looked as if he'd like to do the same to me. He'd promised to have dinner on Christmas Day with his own family, but we made arrangements to meet afterwards.

Anyway, Mam had asked that we not invite anyone to dinner on that particular day. 'It will be our first Christmas without Alice and I'd like it to be just ourselves.'

Our Jean's kids were old enough to understand when she asked them to be quiet. Dad had announced he wanted to say a few words. They sat listening to their grandad when he spoke, though they probably didn't understand what he was saying.

'We were blessed,' Dad said seriously. 'The Good Lord blessed us with an angel in the form of our dear Alice. For some reason He took her from us. It seems a cruel thing to do, but perhaps He had a purpose. And it's not just us who've lost our precious angel, but the hospital too where she saved so many lives. So I'd like you to raise your glass and say goodbye to our Alice. We didn't have her for long, but we were lucky to have her at all.'

We all picked up our glasses. 'Ta-ra, Alice,' we murmured as we sipped our wine.

Of course that wasn't the last time my sister was mentioned in our house, but there was a war on and we had to cope with day-to-day living. We would always miss her, but we were slowly learning how to live without her.

When dinner was over, I was about to help Mam with the washing-up when Ian called. Jean grabbed the tea towel and said she'd do the drying-up.

We went for a walk, Ian and I. There was hardly anyone about, but the pubs were full and everyone was singing. Parties were being held in quite a few houses and inside we could see people wearing paper hats and having a good time.

A tramcar appeared on its way into town and we jumped on it. Straightaway I wished we hadn't. The wrecked streets, the remains of houses without floors or doors, where curtains flapped on broken upstairs windows, was a truly depressing sight to see on Christmas Day. I couldn't stand it any more. It was as if the air raids had reduced the entire city to rubble.

I grabbed Ian's hand. 'Let's go back home,' I said.

He nodded. We got off the tram at the next stop and ran all the way back to Opal Street. Once there, our Jean suggested we sit in the parlour.

'Have some privacy. It's where Dennis and I used to sit years and years ago.' She winked. 'I'll fetch you a cup of tea in a minute and some Christmas cake.'

'It doesn't matter about the cake,' I told her. I'd won the cake in a raffle at Gregg's, but it tasted like cardboard. 'We wouldn't mind some biscuits, though.'

It was in this room we'd eaten our dinner and there was the remains of a fire. In the living room, the wireless was on and a choir was singing 'Away in a Manger'. Our Jean brought the tea, biscuits and two glasses of sherry on a tray.

Once the tea and biscuits were gone, Ian and I sat beside each other on the settee, holding hands and feeling utterly contented. I could have sat there for ever. In the end, I couldn't resist it, and I laid my head on his shoulder.

'It's nice to be home,' he said, squeezing my hand.

'It's nice to have you here,' I replied.

I think it was then that we started kissing. I can't describe just how nice it was. I never wanted him to stop. Then he slid both his arms around me and kissed me even more. I felt the inside of my tummy turn over.

'Let's get married, Amy,' he whispered when the kissing stopped.

I didn't answer straightaway. 'Not yet,' I said after a few moments.

'When then?' he asked.

'I don't know.' I needed to think about it a bit more.

'Then let's get engaged,' he said eagerly. 'We can get a ring the day after tomorrow when the shops open. When I go back to the base, at least I'll have a fiancée if not a wife.'

I swallowed nervously and nodded. 'All right.'

'I love you, Amy.'

I gasped. It was the first time a man had ever told me he loved me. I found it difficult to get my lips around the words, but eventually I said to him, 'And I love you too.'

We stayed cuddled together on the settee until about seven o'clock when Sally came. Jean took the kids home and Dad went fire-watching, not that there were any fires to look out for these days. Ian said he'd better be getting back to his family. It wasn't until he'd gone that I told Mam and Sally about us getting engaged.

This time Mam didn't mind as I was two years older than the first time Ian had proposed.

'Congratulations, girl. What a pity . . .' She stopped and didn't continue. I knew she'd been going to say something about Alice.

Sally looked a bit put out. I suppose it was only natural. We'd been friends for almost all our lives and now Ian had come between us. Though it wasn't as if he would be in Liverpool for long; by this time next week he'd be back in Egypt.

Two days after Christmas, I was on the early shift. Afterwards, I met Ian and we looked in jewellers' shop windows at engagement rings. At the start, I only looked at ones with the tiniest stones, but Ian said he could afford to pay more than I'd thought.

'I can go up to fifteen pounds,' he confided.

'Fifteen!' I was shocked.

'I got money from my grandma for my twenty-first birthday,' he told me. He pointed to a ring in the window. 'How about that one with three stones?'

'I'd like a solitaire,' I said.

I'd never given any thought to engagement rings in the past, but after discussing it with

44

Mam I'd decided a ring with a single diamond would look best.

Half an hour later, a diamond solitaire ring twinkled brightly on the third finger of my left hand. I waved my hand about so that it twinkled even more.

'Thank you, Ian.' I buried my face in his collar. I badly wanted to cry, but perhaps it was only because I was so happy.

We had a meal in Owen Owen's. 'What would you like to do next?' Ian asked when we'd finished.

I knew exactly what I wanted to do next. I'd noticed *Gone With The Wind* was on at the Palais de Luxe cinema in Lime Street. Sally and I had gone to see it when it first came out and ever since I had been longing to see it again. It was nearly four hours long and the best film ever made. I'd fallen in love with Leslie Howard and Sally with Clark Gable.

'Have you seen *Gone With The Wind*?' I asked Ian.

'No, but I've always wanted to.'

'Well, it's on in Lime Street. I've seen it once, but I'd love to go again.'

Ian grinned. 'Then that's where we'll go, Amy.'

I warned him there was to be no necking in the back row and he promised faithfully he would only hold my hand.

For almost the next four hours I forgot I was in a cinema in Liverpool, but imagined myself in the Deep South of America a hundred years ago. I lived the film through the eyes of Scarlett O'Hara, who was so brave and beautiful.

We emerged into the blackout and Ian tried to remember where there was a pub so we could go for a drink. We stood on the pavement of Lime Street in the pitch darkness, waiting for the trams to pass so we could cross to the other side of the road. Ian had remembered there was a pub there. I thought to myself that I didn't really want to spend the rest of my life in Liverpool, living in a little house like our one in Opal Street, having children, then grand-children, until Ian and I were really old. I wanted to be like Scarlett O'Hara and do some-thing exciting with my life, have adventures and fall in love with someone like Leslie Howard.

Then Ian tugged my hand. 'The road is clear, Amy. We can cross now.'

Minutes later, we were in the pub. It was crowded and, like in all pubs nowadays, everyone was singing. I was still feeling a bit sad. Then I thought, what could be more exciting than living through a war and getting engaged to someone like Ian who was years younger than Leslie Howard and better looking if the truth be known? I looked down at my ring. I sighed, not because I was sad, but because I had never felt so content.

Earlier in December, the Japanese air force had destroyed the American fleet as it lay anchored in Pearl Harbor in Hawaii. It was a horrible thing to happen, but it meant that America joined the war on the side of Britain and her allies.

We needed friends. For months, our country had lived in fear of a German invasion. The idea of being invaded, of foreign soldiers marching down our streets, was terrifying.

But now the Americans were coming – Yankee soldiers like those in *Gone With The Wind*.

Ian returned to Egypt, leaving a real ache in my heart. I wore my engagement ring at Gregg's, but only the once. It would have been nice to look at it all day long, but I was worried it would get damaged by the machine I worked on. The other women crowded round during the tea break to admire it.

'What did you and Ian get up to before he went back to Egypt?' one of them asked. She winked suggestively.

I denied that we got up to anything apart from kissing, but she claimed not to believe me.

A lot of the women were really coarse. They used words and said things that I wouldn't dream of putting in my diary. At home, I put my ring back in its little navy-blue velvet box and kept it underneath my pillow.

Chapter Five

I can't say I worried all that much about food rationing. Mam seemed to manage okay with the rations. We ate lots of mince cooked in all sorts of different ways – shepherd's pie, stews, rissoles, Cornish pasties or rolled into meatballs. It wasn't often I felt hungry. We ate eggless sponge cakes without complaint and quite enjoyed the 'pineapple jam' our Jean made out of swedes, a vegetable I normally hated. (A pineapple hadn't been seen in the shops for years.)

No, what bothered me and every other woman I knew was clothes' rationing. We were allowed sixty-six coupons each for a whole year. A coat cost fourteen coupons and a dress eleven. You needed seven for a skirt, and knickers were three. Sixty-six coupons didn't go very far at all. Sally and I wondered how on earth we could make them last a year.

When I came home from work one day Mam showed me this lovely gathered skirt. It was black with a wide band of red-flowered material around the hem.

'It's for you, love,' Mam said with a smile.

'It's really smart,' I gasped. 'Where did it come from? Oh, Mam, let me try it on.'

I tried it on there and then and rushed upstairs to look at myself in the wardrobe mirror. The skirt looked very stylish and fitted perfectly. I rushed back downstairs to Mam.

'I made it,' she said proudly. 'It's only a piece of blackout material.'

Everybody had had to buy the stuff to make special curtains to stop light shining through their old curtains. It could still be bought without coupons.

'Where did the flowered stuff come from?' I asked.

'That's the flowered runner I used to have on the sideboard. I never told anyone how much I disliked it.' Mam looked really pleased with herself. 'I was glad to find a better use for it. Would you like another skirt, love? There's an old blue and white checked tablecloth somewhere that I was going to cut up for dusters. I could use it to decorate a skirt instead.'

'You could make that one for Sally, Mam. She'd be really pleased.'

Mam became quite well known in the area for making clothes out of scraps. People started bringing her their old clothes to see whether she could make something out of them. She was brilliant at turning two old worn summer frocks into one good one. She made a lovely evening skirt for a woman out of a set of faded brocade curtains by using the unfaded bits at the bottom.

She made Sal and me coats out of old grey blankets. I had mine dyed bottle green and Sally had hers dyed dark brown. We bought imitation suede belts for sixpence each from Woolworth's to go with them.

It was a case of make do and mend. It was strange, but we got much more pleasure out of wearing clothes made out of odds and ends than we would have done out of something brand new and costing the earth.

Mum earned quite a lot of money from doing these little jobs for people. She gave every penny to charity.

The Yanks had arrived. They were based in a big army camp in a place called Warrington not far from Liverpool. Their uniform was much smarter than that of the British Army – the lower ranks, that is.

The town centre was full of Yanks, the shops, the cinemas, the theatres and every single restaurant. And, of course, the dances. The Yanks all appeared to be tall, sunburned, handsome and very sure of themselves.

'Got any gum, chum?' the kids would cry whenever they saw a Yank.

Their pockets were full of packets of chewing gum. They threw it to the kids who fought each other to pick it up.

Some girls came into Gregg's and showed off their glossy nylon stockings. 'Got them from a Yank,' they would say with a sly wink.

'What did you have to do for them?' the other women would ask.

'What do you think?' would be the reply.

The best place to meet a Yank was on Central Station in the city centre. This was where the trains came in from Warrington. The Yanks would come pouring off and pick up one of the hundreds of girls waiting for them. One Saturday night, Sally tried to persuade me to go there with her.

I refused. 'I'm engaged to Ian, remember,' I reminded her.

'But you said Ian didn't mind you going out with other chaps,' Sally said.

'I said no such thing,' I cried angrily. 'He said he didn't mind me going dancing, that's all. He trusts me, that's why. Anyway, even if I wasn't engaged to Ian, I wouldn't want some strange man picking me up. He might turn out to be really horrible, Yank or no Yank.'

At that Sally became furious with me. 'You're being really stuck-up, Amy. I suppose you think you're too good to go out with a Yank.'

'I think no such thing.' Perhaps I was fussy, but I didn't care. 'But I do think myself too good to be *picked up* by a Yank, which is a different thing altogether.'

At that point, I went home and Sally went to Central Station.

'I thought you were going dancing,' Mam said when she saw me. 'Or was it to the pictures?'

'It was to a dance. But I've got a bit of a head-ache, Mam,' I lied, though I didn't like lying to my mother. On the other hand, I didn't want to tell her what Sally was up to either.

I spent the evening listening to the wireless, writing a letter to Ian, then bringing my diary up to date, including every word of the argument I'd had with Sally.

On Monday morning on the bus to work, I asked Sally how she'd got on on Saturday.

'I met this chap called Glen who's a cowboy back in America,' she told me.

'A cowboy?' I was impressed. 'Like in the pictures?'

'Yes.' She tossed her head. 'Just like in the pictures. We went to the Tower ballroom in New Brighton. He's a great dancer. He taught me how to jitterbug.'

'Jitterbug?'

'It's a really peculiar way of dancing. He threw me all over the place.'

'Really.' I must say I didn't fancy it myself. 'Are you seeing him again?'

'Yes, on Wednesday. We're going to the pictures. By the way, he's got a mate, Charlie. We could go in a foursome, if you like.'

She looked at me hopefully, but I shook my head. 'I wouldn't dream of going out with another man when I'm engaged to Ian,' I assured her.

'You're too old-fashioned for your own good, Amy Browning,' Sally snapped. 'You're stuck-up, too, and think yourself better than everyone else.'

With that, she got up and sat on another seat. I was upset, but tried not to show it. We didn't speak to each other until coming home on the bus on Friday when she sat beside me once again.

'Glen didn't turn up on Wednesday,' she

said. 'I wondered if you'd like to go to South-port on Saturday, just the two of us. It should be nice now the weather's improving.'

It was April. The daffodils were out in the parks and leaves were appearing on the bare trees.

I agreed straightaway. I didn't like not being friends with Sally. Also I was worried that I was beginning to think too highly of myself, and that I really was becoming stuck-up.

Chapter Six

On Saturday I put on what I called my blackout skirt, with a red cardigan that matched the roses on the hem. I also wore a white beret that Mam had knitted. Sally was just as smartly dressed. I was glad I was friends with her again and looked forward to the day ahead. We planned to visit the fairground in Southport, then go to the pictures to see Veronica Lake and Frederic March in *I Married a Witch*. Afterwards, we were having fish and chips in a proper restaurant, not eating them out of newspaper in the street.

We got off the train at Southport station. Sally said, 'You know, I missed having breakfast. I wouldn't mind a cup of tea and a sticky bun in the station café. Do you fancy one, Amy?'

I wasn't the sort of person to turn down the offer of a cuppa. I agreed straightaway, though I didn't fancy the bun.

The café was almost empty. We sat down near the window and almost immediately two

Yanks came and sat at our table. I was about to tell them to go away when Sally said, 'Amy, this is Glen Morrow and his mate Charlie Kelly.' She laughed gaily at the men. 'Meet my friend Amy Browning.'

I felt a complete fool. And I was so angry that I wanted to burst into tears. In fact, I could feel tears gathering in my eyes and threatening to run down my cheeks.

I said, 'How dare you, Sally?' in a choked voice and jumped to my feet, intending to catch the next train back to Liverpool. Instead, I caught my knee on the wooden table top. It hurt so badly that I fell back in the chair with a cry and rubbed it to take away the pain.

'Didn't you tell Amy we were coming, Sally?'

I had no idea which one was Glen and which was Charlie. The one who spoke had blond hair and dark-brown eyes. His face was tanned a lovely golden colour.

Sally just sniffed and didn't answer.

'That's a pretty lousy thing to do.' The blond one spoke again.

I made another attempt to stand up and this time I managed it. I limped back into the station, but there was nothing showing what time the trains ran or where they were going. The government had taken down road signs and the names of towns and stations, anything that might make life difficult for the Germans, if they invaded.

I was looking around for the ticket office so I could ask about the next train, when a hand rested on my arm.

'I think you should sit down for a while,' the blond-haired soldier said. 'Glen and I have been wandering around and there's a diner just across the way. You and I could go there for a coffee.'

He was obviously Charlie Kelly and he spoke kindly. At the same time, there was a slight smile on his face as if he found the situation rather amusing. Perhaps I was over-reacting, making too much of a fuss.

'Oh, all right,' I said grudgingly.

His hand was still on my arm as he steered me out of the station into the fresh April sunshine. Southport was full of people in their best summer clothes who'd come to spend the day there. Despite the war, the fine weather and the thought that it would soon be summer had made everyone feel cheerful.

To my surprise, the diner he spoke of turned out to be the restaurant of a big posh hotel.

'A pot of coffee for two,' he said to the elderly waiter.

We both sank into dark-red velvet chairs. The coffee arrived in a silver pot on a silver tray. The cups and saucers were eggshell-thin china.

'Cream, madam?' the waiter asked as he poured the coffee.

'Yes, please,' I stammered.

We sometimes had cream at home, but it came out of a tin. We'd never had the sort you could pour from a jug before.

'I can't remember if your friend told us your surname or not,' Charlie said.

'It's Browning,' I replied. 'Amy Browning.'

'I'm Charlie Kelly,' he said.

I nodded. 'I'd gathered that much.'

To my astonishment, he went down on one knee on the thick carpet and took my hand. 'Will Miss Amy Browning kindly agree to spend the next few hours in Southport with Mr Charlie Kelly?'

I frowned suspiciously. 'Are you sure you didn't know I was coming with Sally?'

'No.' He put his other hand on his chest. 'Cross my heart and hope to die,' he said firmly. 'I intended staying with Glen and Sally until after we'd been to the fair, then exploring this pleasant little town on my own. But it looks as if an extremely pretty young lady is also going to be on her own and it would be great if she were agreeable to exploring the pleasant little town with me.'

The waiter and the man and woman on the next table were looking at us and smiling. In the end, I had to laugh. I couldn't help it. He looked so daft, yet so sincere.

'Oh, all right,' I said. 'I'll come with you.'

He sat back in the chair, pleased with himself. 'It's not eleven o'clock yet,' he said, 'and today has already turned out much better than expected.'

We decided to avoid the fairground because I didn't want to come face to face with Sally. I would have to think hard about whether or not I still wanted her as a friend. We went to the beach, which was as flat and as smooth as silk. The tide had gone out and the sand was glistening in the sunshine. The waters of the Irish Sea shone like melting silver in the distance.

Charlie linked my arm in his and told me about his life back in the United States. He was twenty-three and he came from Sacramento, where the sun shone most of the time and the flowers were as big as footballs. When the war started he and his best pal, Howard, had been helping Howard's dad with his decorating business. He still hadn't made up his mind what he'd like to do with the rest of his life.

'Sacramento is a wonderful city, Amy. It's the capital of California and a truly great place to live. Mind you, when I go back home I might well spend a bit of time in Los Angeles and see how the Hollywood crowd live.'

'Hollywood!' I could hardly believe my ears. He was actually talking about Hollywood, which could have been on another planet as far as I was concerned.

'Yeah.' His brown eyes shone. 'I don't want to be a film star or anything like that. But it'd be interesting to see how movies are made. I'm a keen photographer. I wish I'd brought my camera with me today. I'd like to watch and see how the professionals do it.'

He still lived with his mam and dad, his sister Janet and his brother Sean. He showed me a photo of his family who were all smiling happily.

'Dad runs a grocery store. He wants Sean and me to take over when he retires. But I've no intention of spending the rest of my life in such a boring job.'

'How about Sean?' I asked. 'What does he think?'

'Sean's fifteen. His only interest is playing baseball.'

The tide was coming in, racing towards us in little waves. We turned and walked back to the promenade. Charlie said he'd quite like to visit the pier. 'Do they have pinball machines there?'

'I think so. We call them slot machines.'

I'd played on them loads of times in Southport and New Brighton, but had never won a penny that I hadn't immediately lost again.

'Anyway, Amy, how about you?' Charlie said warmly. 'It's about time you told me about yourself. You've listened to me all this time. Now it's your turn.'

'I work on a drilling machine in a munitions factory,' I told him.

At this, he looked amazed. 'I thought that was a man's job?'

'It used to be. It'll probably be the same in America soon. The men will join up and the women will take over their jobs.'

'Good thing too,' Charlie said approvingly, squeezing my arm.

I told him about my family and about our Alice having been killed in the air raids. Her photo was the only one I carried in my handbag. I showed it to Charlie. He stared at it for a long time before saying, 'She was a very beautiful young lady.' He handed it back with a sigh.

I don't know why, but I didn't mention Ian. I wasn't wearing my engagement ring. I hadn't forgotten to put it on, but whenever I wore it I was worried the diamond would drop out.

Now I was worried about something else. Why didn't I want Charlie to know I was engaged? I felt as if I was being disloyal to Ian by pretending he didn't exist.

Then Charlie asked straight out, 'Have you got a boyfriend, Amy?'

'No.' I felt terrible. I was a truly horrible person. God really should have left our Alice and taken me. I doubt whether Alice had told a lie in her life.

Charlie stopped walking and looked right into my eyes. 'That's good, honey,' he said.

Honey. It was the first time I'd been called honey. I hoped it wouldn't be the last.

A strange feeling spread over me when Charlie once again linked my arm in his. I am finding it hard to describe in my diary. It was as if butterflies were dancing in my stomach. It felt awfully nice. I caught my breath and realised that I was already a little bit in love with Charlie Kelly who I'd only known for a few hours. I also knew that I'd never felt this way about Ian. Yet I'd known him all my life and intended to marry him one day.

I'm pleased to say there was no sign of Sally and Glen on the pier. Not only that but I won five pence on a machine, although I lost it again on another machine. Charlie won quite a few shillings, which he offered to me.

'No, thanks. I'll only lose them as well.' I pointed to the rifle range. 'Are you any good at that?'

'I'm not just good at it, Amy. I'm a first-class shot.'

He dragged me across to the stall. The prizes were teddy bears with a ribbon tied around their necks.

Within minutes, he'd won two teddy bears with different coloured ribbons. The man in charge of the range didn't look all that pleased.

'Let those little girls have them,' I said to Charlie when he went to give the bears to me. I didn't fancy spending the rest of the day carrying them around. The girls had been watching him wide-eyed and full of admiration.

We left the pier, had a cup of tea and a sandwich, then went to see *Babes on Broadway* with Judy Garland. I'd been looking forward to *I Married a Witch*, but once again I didn't want to come face to face with Sally. Not that I minded. Judy Garland was possibly my very favourite woman film star.

Afterwards, we went back to the hotel where we'd had coffee that morning and this time we had a proper meal, of beef with onion gravy and roast potatoes.

I was beginning to wonder how I could explain what had happened today to Mam. In the end, I decided to tell the truth. I would describe the trick Sally had played on me.

'It was how I met Charlie,' I would say. I knew Mam wouldn't mind my spending all day with him when I told her what he was like.

We came out of the hotel and went into the station so that I could catch my train home. By now it was dark. Charlie found a porter who said the next train to Liverpool wasn't for another half-hour. Charlie said he would catch the same train and get off in the centre of Liverpool. We found a waiting room with blackout on the windows. Candles flickered on a table in the middle of the room. There were two other couples there.

We sat down and Charlie put his arm around me. 'Can I see you again?' he whispered in my ear.

I'd known this might happen, but had no idea what to say. I mumbled something I couldn't understand myself.

'It wouldn't be for a week or so,' Charlie was saying. 'Tomorrow I'm going to London with Colonel Dryden. I learned to speak a few languages at college and I'll be translating for the colonel at a meeting with some French military folk.'

I mumbled something else. Charlie seemed to know what I was saying more than I did myself. He went on, 'Give me your address, honey, and I'll write when I get back.'

'All right,' I said at last. He gave me a piece of paper and I wrote down my address. I could only just see in the dark.

We sat in silence while we waited. It was a comfortable silence. I wasn't wondering what to say next.

It was as dark on the train as it was outside. The windows hadn't been blacked out and it was like travelling through a never-ending tunnel. When someone struck a match, a man shouted, 'Put that light out. It can be seen from the air.' The light vanished.

Every now and then Charlie would whisper in my ear. I could feel his breath warm on my cheek and I would whisper back.

'Yes, it has been the best day of my life too,' I agreed. Yes, I couldn't wait to see him again.

The train stopped at my station. Charlie kissed me on the cheek and I got off. I walked home in a dream. The day was almost over. Nothing would ever be quite the same again.

Chapter Seven

As it was a Saturday, Dad had gone to the pub, but when I got home Mam had a visitor. I could hear them talking when I opened the door. The visitor sounded really posh.

'This is our Amy,' Mam said when I went into the living room. 'Amy, love, this is Dorothy Gray. She's from London and she's lodging with the Brandreths across the street.'

Dorothy Gray was a little older than me. She looked extremely smart with short black hair and a thick fringe. Her frock was pale blue with white embroidery on the yoke. It looked as if it had cost the earth. So did her white shoes with low, narrow heels.

'How do you do, Amy?'

We shook hands. Since getting an engagement ring, I'd begun to look at other women's hands to see whether they were wearing a ring. Dorothy not only wore a ring with a massive ruby stone and a diamond on either side, but a wedding ring too.

'What are you doing in Liverpool?' I asked.

I had planned on going straight to bed to think about Charlie. But it seemed rude to rush off. Anyway, what little I'd seen of Dorothy I quite liked.

'I've been transferred from London to manage the Liverpool branch of the Royal Oxford bank,' she replied in her very refined voice.

'Imagine,' Mam said, butting in, 'a woman managing a bank. And one so young as well.' Dorothy, it appeared, was twenty-five.

'I wouldn't be surprised,' Dorothy said modestly, 'if I'm not the first female bank manager in Great Britain.'

On Monday I was on the early shift. Sally didn't turn up for the bus to work, nor did she the next day. I discovered she had changed shifts. From now on, she would work the opposite shift to me.

I was angry with Sally, but we had been friends since we were five. Now we were twenty and I thought it might do us good not to see each other for a while. I wondered how she'd got on with Glen in Southport and whether they'd had as good a time as Charlie and me. After some thought, I reckoned that was impossible. Charlie and I had enjoyed a perfect day.

I still had someone to go to the pictures with. I discovered that Dorothy Gray was a real film fan. Two days after we met, we went to see *I Married a Witch* in town. We even made arrangements to go dancing at the Grafton on Saturday.

'Of course, I can't make a date with a chap or let one take me home,' Dorothy said. 'My husband, Brian, would have a fit.'

Brian was an officer in the Royal Navy. Dorothy had no idea which part of the world he was in. He wasn't allowed to tell her in his letters.

She went on, 'You, being engaged, are in the same position, aren't you?'

I agreed. Mam had told her about Ian being my fiancé. So far, I hadn't mentioned Charlie Kelly to a soul. With Dorothy being there when I got back from Southport, Mam hadn't asked what sort of day I'd had.

A week later I was expecting a letter from Charlie. By then, I was working the afternoon shift and would be home when the letter arrived. I hoped Mam would be out shopping when it came. If she was in, she was bound to ask who it was from.

And what was I supposed to tell her? I had absolutely no idea.

It turned out I had no need to worry. The weeks passed and Charlie's promised letter didn't arrive. At first, I was heartbroken. I cried myself to sleep night after night, my head under the bedclothes so no one would hear. I thought I had met the love of my life and that Charlie had too. But it seems that I was wrong.

After a month or so, my heartbreak turned into a feeling of relief. Had Charlie written, had we got involved, there would have been all sorts of problems. I would have hated to hurt Ian, who I did love in a nice, quiet sort of way. I've no idea how Mam and Dad would have felt about me going out with an American, let alone marrying him one day and moving thousands of miles away.

So I suppose it was best for everyone concerned that things had turned out the way they had.

Mam was determined to do something special for my birthday in September.

'It's your twenty-first,' she said, as if I didn't know. 'We must have a party or go out to dinner in town.'

'I'd sooner we went to dinner.'

I wasn't in the mood for a party. Anyway, there weren't all that many friends I could invite. Quite a few were married and had children. Or, due to the war, they'd gone to work in other parts of the country. One or two had joined the forces. The girl who'd sat in front of me in class had been killed in an air raid. I hadn't seen Sally, my best friend of all, since that day in Southport.

'Dinner it is, then,' Mam agreed. 'I'll talk it over with your father and we'll book a table somewhere. I wonder whether Dennis will be home to come with our Jean. And we'll invite Grandad, of course. Should I ask Dorothy, love?'

'Yes, please.'

Mam approved of Dorothy taking the place of Sally as my best friend.

My birthday party became a much bigger occasion than expected. The reason for this was that, early in July, Ian wrote to say he was being transferred to an airbase in Norfolk on the east coast. He was to take a course on being an engine fitter. Once trained, he would stay in the area. Planes took off daily from the east coast to bomb Germany.

'Why don't we get married?' he said in his

letter. He even drew a line underneath the words. 'We could do it on your birthday.'

I read this part of the letter to Mam.

'Do you really want to marry Ian, love?' she asked gently.

'I think so,' I said hesitantly.

'You don't sound very sure, Amy. If you love him, you should want to marry him very much.'

I sighed. 'Do you like him, Mam?'

'He's a lovely young man,' she replied, nodding approvingly, 'and he'll make a good husband. He's already got a trade and you'll never go hungry being married to a tradesman. Your dad will gladly agree to you getting wed to Ian Taylor. Mind you, Amy love,' she went on, 'it's your opinion that matters, not ours.'

'I know,' I said faintly.

I could only imagine what she would have said about my marrying Charlie Kelly. Still, there was no chance of Charlie Kelly coming back into my life.

I nodded. 'I would very much like to marry Ian, Mam.'

'Then you'd better write and tell him. Your dad'll be pleased. Tomorrow, I'll pop round to see his mam to discuss the wedding arrangements.'

I insisted I didn't want many guests. Although

Mam's relatives in Ireland wouldn't be coming, Dad's family, who lived near us, would have to be invited. Close friends of Mam and Dad who'd known me all my life would be offended if they didn't receive an invitation. And of course we'd have to include Ian's parents, his two married brothers and his sister, Pamela, who was single. He also had various aunts and uncles who would have to be asked. Before I knew it there were nearly fifty guests.

'Don't fuss, love,' Mam said when I complained. 'You only get married once. A wedding isn't just for the bride and groom, anyway. It's for all sorts of other folk too.'

And here was me thinking the bride and groom were the only people that mattered.

I arrived at Gregg's one afternoon and came face to face with Sally in the cloakroom. I was shocked at how sick she looked. Her face was as white as a ghost.

I was glad that we had the opportunity to speak to each other. 'What are you doing here, Sal?' I asked.

'I'm waiting to see Miss Mitchell,' she said.

Miss Mitchell was the Welfare Officer. She looked after the women workers, arranging lodgings for those who didn't live in Liverpool.

She found doctors when they were needed and sorted out problems for women who were unable to sort them out themselves.

'Is something wrong?' I asked Sally now. I wasn't being nosy. I couldn't think of what else to say.

The cloakroom was crowded. The women from the morning shift were taking off their overalls and the afternoon shift were putting theirs on.

I was surprised when tears appeared in my old friend's eyes. 'Oh, Amy,' she whispered. 'I'm in the club, having a baby. Miss Mitchell is looking for a place where I can go to have it.'

'Oh, heck, Sal. I'm so sorry.'

I felt as if I wanted to cry myself. I wanted to ask who the father was, but it was none of my business.

'If you hadn't gone home that day in Southport, Amy, if we'd all stayed together, it wouldn't have happened,' Sally said accusingly. 'As it was, Glen took advantage of me being on my own.'

She hadn't realised that I'd remained in Southport with Charlie. So Glen was the father of her baby and she was trying to blame me for her getting pregnant. In a way, I didn't care if thinking it made her feel better.

'Does Glen know?' I asked.

'I haven't seen him since that day.' She looked terribly unhappy. 'I haven't told my mam and dad yet. The baby will start to show soon and they'll bloody kill me when they find out. If Miss Mitchell finds me a place, I might leave home without telling them.'

'I'm really sorry, Sal,' I said again. 'Write to me from wherever you are and I'll write back.'

'You can send me a slice of wedding cake,' she said bitterly. 'I heard you were marrying Ian. You don't know how lucky you are, Amy. Everything goes right for you.'

Only because I don't put myself in the position where they can go wrong, I could have said. But I didn't want to say things that would only make her even more unhappy.

Someone nudged me and said, 'C'mon, Amy. You'll be late.'

I was putting on my overalls and when I turned round Sally was no longer there.

That weekend, I went round to Coral Street to see her.

Her mother answered the door. 'Is Sally in?' I asked.

'She's gone away,' Mrs Clarke snapped and slammed the door in my face.

Chapter Eight

Ian came home in August. He lifted me up and kissed me so tenderly that I couldn't help but kiss him back the same way. After telling me how much he loved me about half a dozen times, he asked how the wedding plans were going.

'Dorothy Gray, you haven't met her, but she lives across the street, is lending me her wedding dress. Oh, it's lovely, Ian,' I cried.

It had been made by a dressmaker in London who made clothes for actresses and other famous women. Dorothy was a size bigger than me, but her mother was taking it in a bit so it would fit.

'I just know you'll look beautiful in it, love.' Ian stroked my hair.

'Oh, and you'll never guess, Mam's already made a wedding cake, but because of the war you're not allowed to have icing as it uses up too much sugar. But,' I continued, 'you can hire a cardboard wedding cake to put on top of your own one, so at least it looks good at the reception.'

Ian laughed out loud. 'Where shall we go on our honeymoon?' he asked.

'Honeymoon? Will you get enough leave for us to have a honeymoon?'

'I'm being allowed five whole days.'

'Could we go to London?'

Dorothy had told me all about the big shops and the famous sights like Trafalgar Square and Piccadilly Circus. She told me that the king and queen still lived in Buckingham Palace, despite the recent air raids. 'They refused to go and live somewhere safer.'

'There's loads and loads of places there that I'd love to see,' I told Ian.

'London it is,' he said. 'I'll find out about a hotel.'

For the first time I began to really look forward to my wedding.

That night Margery and Reg, Ian's mam and dad, came round to our house and we made yet more plans for the day. Margery was a nice, outsized lady with a heavily powdered face. For a middle-aged man, Reg was very good looking. I hoped Ian would look as handsome as his dad when he was fifty. Right now, Ian was grinning at me from across the room.

'I hope you don't mind, Amy,' Margery said at the start, 'but despite our Pamela having two married brothers, she's still never managed to be a bridesmaid. Would you mind if she was a bridesmaid at your wedding? She'd be ever so pleased. I'll see to her dress, of course.'

I liked Ian's sister, Pamela. She worked in a factory, just like me, but on the other side of Liverpool. I said I'd love for her to be my bridesmaid.

'I've already asked our Jean's little girl, Emily to be one,' I said. 'She's only five.'

'Has she got a dress yet?' Margery asked.

I shook my head. 'Jean's been looking for some nice material.'

Ian's mam looked delighted. 'I've got a wine-coloured bedspread that was a silver wedding present and has never been used. There's enough material there for two bridesmaids' frocks, particularly with one being small.'

'I'd be willing to make them,' my own mam said.

'She's a first-class dressmaker,' my dad said in support.

'Oh, well, that's settled.' Margery gave a satis-fied smile.

*

Later on Ian and I went for a walk.

'It's supposed to be *our* wedding,' I said, 'but nobody asked us a thing. I mean, what makes them think I want wine-coloured bridesmaids' frocks?'

Ian frowned. 'Don't you like that colour, love?'

I laughed. 'I don't mind a bit. It's just that it would have been nice to have been asked for my opinion.'

It was only then I remembered that Sally and I had always promised to be each other's bridesmaid when we got married.

'Though whoever gets married first will be matron of honour, at the other's wedding,' Sally had said. 'I wonder which one of us it'll be?'

Now it was me getting married first, while Sally was away somewhere having a baby.

An upstairs room was booked for the reception in the King's Arms, Dad's favourite pub, which was just around the corner from our house. As the church was around another corner, it meant we could walk everywhere and didn't need wedding cars. They were difficult to get, anyway, as petrol was rationed. I hoped and prayed it wouldn't rain on the day.

Getting married in wartime wasn't easy. There was a shortage of everything. The government kindly allowed extra food points for each guest, though only enough for forty. It was my job to call at the local Food Office to collect the points. The women guests had been asked to bring a loaf of bread each. Two of our neighbours would make the sandwiches while the wedding ceremony was taking place.

Dorothy's mother sent the altered wedding dress from London. It was made of the softest off-white silk with a lace collar and cuffs. It fitted perfectly. Mam still had her own veil, which our Jean had worn and which would now be passed on to me.

'I'd always imagined our Alice wearing it too,' Mam said with a sigh.

Margery and Reg offered to pay for the flowers. I would carry a bouquet of red roses, while the bridesmaids would have white. Tiny sprays of rosebuds had been ordered for the guests' lapels and buttonholes.

The King's Arms, as a favour to one of their regular customers, had provided a small barrel of beer, while Grandad had given the bride and groom a bottle of champagne as a present.

Bottles of wine, sherry and port had been promised on the day.

Everything was running smoothly and according to plan when, on the Monday before we were due to be married on the Saturday, a telegram arrived from Ian.

ALL LEAVE CANCELLED, it said. CAN WE GET MARRIED TOMORROW? HAVE TO BE BACK MIDDAY WEDNESDAY. LOVE, IAN.

'What is it, love?' Mam was standing in the hall behind me. Her voice shook. She must have thought the telegram had brought bad news about our Harry.

'It's all right, Mam.' I gave her a quick hug. 'It's addressed to me.'

I showed her the telegram and she gave a little scream. 'It's much too late to make arrangements to get married tomorrow.'

'Maybe so, but I mean to try, Mam,' I said firmly. I pushed her into a chair when she looked as if she was about to have hysterics.

I was on the afternoon shift and due to leave for Gregg's in half an hour. I quickly decided not to go in that day. It would be the first shift I'd missed since I'd started work there nearly three years ago.

'If any of the guests have a telephone, I'll give them a ring from the Post Office.'

I was talking to myself as much as Mam. I'd make a list in a minute and while I was there I'd ring Gregg's, too.

'Otherwise I'll send telegrams. If people can't come, then it's just too bad. Then I'll go wherever you're supposed to go and get a special marriage licence.'

'I think you'd better get the licence first. The office might close early.' Mam had quickly become her old, sensible self again. 'I'll run round and see Margery, tell her what's happened.' Margery worked as a clerk in the local police station. 'Maybe they'll give her some time off to come home. After all, it's for her own son's wedding.'

It was gone midnight by the time Mam, Dad and I went to bed. Everything had been done that needed to be done. The special licence had been obtained and we were getting married at half past two at St James's church. The bridesmaids' frocks had been pressed. The cardboard wedding cake had been borrowed from the local baker. I wouldn't have a bouquet of red roses but the florist had promised to see what she could do. The King's Arms was still available.

We had no idea how many guests would turn

up tomorrow. Some had sent back telegrams, telling us whether or not they could come. Others had probably not found their telegram until they arrived home from work that evening. By then, the Post Office would have closed so they wouldn't have been able to send a reply in time.

I woke up in the morning to a dull, wet day. But by the time I'd got up and had a good wash, the sun was struggling to come out. It emerged in all its glory at around eight o'clock. I had planned on having my hair set at the hairdresser's, but ended up doing it myself.

Dorothy had come earlier to wish me good luck. Sadly, she couldn't possibly take a day off without telling someone a whole week before.

'It's so they have time to arrange for another manager to take over,' she said and kissed my cheek. 'I hope you and Ian have a lovely day. Next time we meet, you'll be a married woman.'

My stomach turned a cartwheel at the thought.

At around ten, Pamela, Ian's sister, arrived. There'd been so many knocks on the door that morning that Mam had left it open for people to come straight in. Pamela had come to tell us that Ian had hitchhiked from Norfolk over-night and was fast asleep at home.

'He was about to come round and tell you himself,' she said breathlessly, having run all the way, 'but Mam and I stopped him just in time. I mean, the bridegroom's not supposed to see the bride on the day of the wedding until they're in church, are they? It's meant to be unlucky.'

'No. Anyway, I wouldn't want him seeing me with my hair all wet and me still in my dressing gown. It might put him off getting married.'

Pamela giggled. 'I doubt that, Amy.'

'Hello,' a voice called from the hall. It was the florist with the flowers. 'All we could get was carnations,' the woman explained. 'And then only pink, but we have plenty of fern. Oh, and can we have the silver paper back, please? We can't get it for love nor money these days. I'll come for it tomorrow.'

Chapter Nine

My dad came home from work just after one. He'd had a dirty job on the docks that morning. I was banished upstairs while the tin bath was brought in from the yard and Mam boiled water for him to get bathed in.

Anyway, it was time for me to put my dress on. Our Jean came with the kids. Dennis, her husband, was away at sea again.

'He misses everything,' she sighed.

Mickey jumped up and down on Mam and Dad's bed while Emily admired herself in the wardrobe mirror. She looked so pretty in the bridesmaid's dress made from a wine-coloured bedspread.

I sat in front of the dressing-table mirror while Jean arranged my hair. She finished by placing the little circle of silk flowers and pearls that Ian's mam had worn at her wedding on top of my brown curls.

'They say that brides should wear something old, something new, something borrowed, something blue,' she remarked when she'd finished.

'Nearly everything I'm wearing is either borrowed or old,' I said to her. 'My silk stockings are new, but I haven't got anything blue.'

We were searching for something blue when Emily remembered she had a blue handkerchief tucked up her sleeve. I tucked it up my sleeve instead.

'There!' Jean said when I was completely ready. 'You look lovely, Sis.'

Afterwards, I could hardly remember what happened at my wedding. I recalled Ian in his air force uniform, waiting for me in front of the altar as I walked up the aisle on Dad's arm. I recalled the feel of the wedding ring as Ian slipped it on to the third finger of my left hand. I only faintly recollect drinking Grandad's champagne at the reception and it tickling my nose.

Mam told me later that about half the guests turned up and they all really enjoyed themselves.

For my going-away outfit, I'd bought a really smart costume from C & A Modes. It was powder blue with a straight skirt and fitted jacket. I thought I wouldn't have the opportunity to wear it, because Ian had to return to his unit tomorrow and the honeymoon in London had been cancelled. In fact, I was wondering where we'd sleep on our first night together. I didn't fancy sleeping at either our house or his parents'.

I was therefore surprised when he informed me he'd booked a room for us at the Adelphi in town. Now the Adelphi is the poshest hotel in Liverpool. Really famous people stay there. I'd never thought I would set foot inside its doors, let alone sleep there.

So, at six o'clock, I changed into my blue costume. We left the reception, where everyone was having a marvellous time, and caught a tram into town. At the Adelphi, Ian carried me over the threshold into our room.

I don't know whether anyone will ever read this diary. In case they do, I'd sooner leave out what happened on the first night I spent with my new husband. All I will say is that I enjoyed it quite a lot and it didn't hurt nearly as much as I expected.

Next morning, I went to Lime Street station with Ian to see him off on the train.

'Why was your leave cancelled?' I asked. In all the excitement, I hadn't thought to ask before.

'There's a real bigwig visiting on Saturday and

we've all got to be there,' he replied. 'Everyone thinks it might be Churchill.' He took me in his arms. 'I won't stop thinking about you every minute of every day,' he whispered. 'I love you, Amy, more than I can say.'

'And I love you,' I said softly. 'I wish you didn't have to go away.'

The train doors were being slammed. Ian struggled into a crowded carriage. He would have to stand all the way to Birmingham where he would change trains. He looked so young and so incredibly nice that I felt a pang of love that really hurt.

He opened a window and blew me a kiss. I blew one back.

Then the train chugged out of the station, blowing smoke everywhere. I waved to my new husband until the train disappeared around a bend.

I left the station feeling terribly sad. As it was Wednesday and half-day closing, not a single shop was open. I wandered around the empty city, becoming sadder and sadder. After a while, I remembered I was working the afternoon shift at Gregg's. Despite still wearing my going-away outfit, I caught a bus to the factory. In the cloakroom, I changed into my overalls and tied a scarf around my hair.

Quite a few of the women shouted 'Amy!' when I went into the workshop.

'I thought you were getting married today?' one of them called.

'No, it was yesterday,' I answered.

'Poor girl, you didn't get a honeymoon, did you?'

I really don't know why I started crying, but I did. I just stood there and cried and cried. I was helped into the First Aid room where I cried even more. The nurse took my pulse, made me a cup of tea and sat me in a comfortable chair. She gave me two aspirins and told me to close my eyes and try to relax.

I'm not sure how long I sat there, but after a while I began to feel better. The nurse took my pulse again and said it had slowed down. I could go back to work if I wanted.

I returned to the workshop where everyone made an enormous fuss of me. In the canteen at teatime, the foreman, Alf Cutler, presented me with a lovely china teaset, a present from everyone in the workshop.

'You weren't supposed to get this 'til Friday,' he said, 'but nothing can be relied on during a war. Dates don't mean anything any more.'

I went home feeling my old self again, but it

didn't last for long. On Saturday, a letter came for me from Charlie Kelly.

It had happened four months ago on the day after we had met in Southport. He'd been travelling to London when the car he was in had skidded off the road into a ditch.

'I was unconscious for the next two days,' he wrote. His writing was large and untidy and I found it hard to read. 'When I came to, both my legs were broken.'

A few days later, he'd been flown to a military hospital in Washington. His letter went on:

'The paper with your address on had been in my jacket pocket, but had been lost somewhere. I wrote to Glen Morrow, you know, the guy who went out with your friend, Sally. But he hadn't seen her since that day in Southport.'

It had been ages before he could walk properly again. Then he'd been allowed to stay with his folks in Sacramento for a few weeks before returning to Britain.

'I'm now back at the base in Warrington. The first thing I was given was a bag of stuff out of my old locker. And what should I find in it, Amy, but your address. It hadn't been in my pocket, after all. So, honey, when can we meet? I can't wait to see you again.'

Chapter Ten

On Saturday mornings, Mam always met her friend, Rita Shearer. They'd go for a cup of tea and a scone in Reilly's Restaurant on the Dock Road. As for my dad, he worked hard all week and stayed in bed until it was time for the pubs to open.

So when Charlie's letter came I was able to read it in peace. I wouldn't let myself wonder whether I'd have still married Ian if I'd known what had happened to Charlie. I just knew I had to write back to him straightaway. If he wasn't told I was married, he could well turn up at the house looking for me.

I went upstairs, taking with me a pen and ink, a writing pad and an envelope. Using my diary as a desk, I dipped the pen in the ink and wrote, 'Dear Charlie . . .'

I leaned back against the headboard and tried to think what to put next. I had to get it right first time, not waste pages from a precious writing pad in wartime. They were really hard to get nowadays.

In the end, all I wrote was, 'I'm sorry about your accident and hope you are completely better. Earlier this week, I got married and am no longer Amy Browning, but Amy Taylor. I loved meeting you, Charlie, but am afraid I can never see you again. Yours sincerely, Amy.'

I was about to fold the letter, but stopped. Should I mention that Sally was having Glen's baby? I thought for a long time, but eventually I decided not to say anything. Glen hadn't been interested enough in Sally to see her again. I decided to leave things as they were. I knew I would spend the rest of my life wondering whether I had done the right thing.

I addressed the envelope, placed the letter inside and put it in my handbag. When I went out that afternoon I'd buy a stamp and post it.

These days the war seems very far away. The air raids have stopped. We got used to food and clothes rationing, and the blackout. Things like electric fires, light bulbs, candles, hairclips, umbrellas and dozens of other things have disappeared from the shops. Our Harry sent short, very dull letters from India. We didn't care about the letters as long as he was alive and not in danger.

I still bought the *Daily Mirror* every day. The

news wasn't good. Our side was losing an awful lot of men, either killed or taken prisoner. But the idea that Britain might *lose* the war didn't bear thinking about.

At the beginning of November, two months after I'd married Ian, there was an announcement on the BBC. We were asked to stay up until midnight when we would hear good news.

We stayed up, Mam, Dad and me. The news was that, in Egypt, the Germans were in full retreat. We were winning at last.

Winston Churchill, the Prime Minister, made a speech. 'This is not the end,' he said. 'It is not even the beginning of the end. But it is perhaps the end of the beginning.'

I thought that was very, very clever.

By the time I heard Churchill's speech, I had realised I was almost certainly expecting Ian's baby. I had missed two periods, yet had always been very regular. It meant that by next June I would be a mother. Me, Amy Browning – no, Amy Taylor – a mother.

A few days later I wrote and told Ian, and the same night I told Mam. To my surprise, she burst into tears.

'Oh, if only our Alice was still alive to look

after you,' she sobbed. 'She helped our Jean with both her babies.'

I put my arm around her shoulders. 'It would have been nice, Mam,' I said. 'I'll just have to attend the antenatal clinic like other women.'

It meant I would have to leave Gregg's. Women weren't allowed to work on the machines if they were pregnant. I'd wait until after Christmas to tell everyone.

Christmas passed in a blur. Ian came home, but he only had a forty-eight-hour pass, which meant he'd hardly been in Liverpool for more than a few hours when it was time for him to return to the air force base on the other side of the country.

I felt really miserable when I left Gregg's. I'd enjoyed my time there and had made loads of good friends that I would miss. I had intended going to work part-time for a few months, but Mam decided it was time *she* went to work.

'It's about time I did my bit towards the war effort. And I'd sooner you took things easy, love. There's no need for you to look for another job.'

She went to work as a cook in the restaurant on Lime Street station. It didn't pay much, but as the wife of a serviceman I was getting an allowance from the Royal Air Force. I would get even more when my baby was born. Our family wouldn't be hard up.

I went for a walk along the Dock Road every morning. When I came home I would sit in Mam's chair. I was growing bigger and bigger by the day. I knitted baby cardigans, booties and mittens, and tried not to think about Charlie Kelly. At around four, I would go into the kitchen and start making the tea.

Our Jean came to see me a couple of times a week. Mickey, who was now three, would put his ear against my tummy and said he could feel my baby kick. It made me dizzy thinking about the real live child inside me. Jean held a sewing needle suspended from a piece of cotton over my tummy. When it went round clockwise Jean announced that the baby was a boy.

'No,' Mam said when she came home. 'If it turns clockwise it's a girl. Anyway, it's just an old wives' tale and doesn't mean a thing. I did it when I was expecting you four kids and it was wrong every time.'

I said I didn't care whether I had a boy or a girl and neither did Ian.

I had loads of visitors apart from Jean. Girls

from Gregg's often turned up after work when they were on the morning shift. Neighbours dropped in from time to time. Some nights Dorothy and I went to the pictures. Every few weeks I went to the clinic where the nurses said I was doing fine. The nearest maternity hospital was expecting me in the middle of June. Everything was going smoothly.

Chapter Eleven

There was a knock on the front door one morning in May. I'd just got home from my walk. These days they were rather slow and gentle. I was huge and became breathless easily.

To save me getting up to let visitors in, Mam usually left the door on the latch. I shouted, 'Come in, whoever you are.'

Usually, the visitor would say their name after opening the door, but this time nothing was said. All I heard were footsteps before a strange woman entered the room. She was very attractive with long black hair and silvery-grey eyes. Her clothes looked really expensive.

'Are you related to Alice Browning?' she asked. She had an accent, either Scottish or Irish, but I wasn't sure.

'I'm her sister,' I replied. 'Who are you?'

'I'm Noreen MacDonald. My husband, Brian, worked with your sister at Mossley Hill Hospital.'

'I think I remember her mentioning a Dr MacDonald,' I said.

'Do you indeed?' she said in an odd tone of voice.

She removed something from a tan leather handbag that looked as expensive as her clothes. When she held it in front of me I saw it was a bundle of letters. I guessed there were about a dozen held together with an elastic band.

'These are from your sister to my husband,' she said.

'Really?' The exact meaning of her words escaped me for the moment.

'My husband died as a result of the same bomb that killed your sister.' Her face was angry. I couldn't understand why, instead of being upset, she looked so cross.

'I'm awfully sorry,' I said. I was still feeling a bit confused.

'It's almost two years since he died. But it's only lately that I've felt up to going through his clothes. I thought there must be other men who could make use of them. I found these,' she waved the letters, 'on a shelf in his wardrobe hidden behind his shirts.' She looked even angrier. 'They are love letters from your sister to my husband.'

I gasped. 'Alice would never—'

Before I could go any further, she interrupted me. 'Alice would never do such a thing because she was so pure and innocent? Except she wasn't,' she cried harshly. 'If you read the letters you will see she was having an affair with my husband. They were lovers. They stayed together in hotels. Do your parents live here?' she asked suddenly.

'Yes.'

'Then kindly give them the letters to read.' She threw the bundle on to the table. 'Maybe they'll change their opinion of their beloved daughter. She was nothing but a bitch, a two-timing bitch who was trying to steal my husband.'

With that, Noreen MacDonald turned around and left the room. I could hear her sobbing as she ran down the hall. Seconds later, the front door slammed.

I sat there, unable to move, for quite a few minutes. Then I took a deep breath and reached for the letters. I removed the elastic band and glanced through them. Only the one word, 'Brian', was written on the front of each envelope. I recognised our Alice's neat, clear writing.

On impulse, I put the envelope against my lips and kissed the word that my beloved sister had written. I thought no less of her for having had an affair. But knowing would upset Mam and Dad with their old-fashioned views.

Dad always left the fire laid, ready for me to light if it turned cold. I hadn't lit it for weeks, mainly to save fuel, which was difficult to get. I picked up the matches and decided to light it today.

I had no intention of reading my sister's letters to her lover or to let anyone else read them. As the fire took hold, I put them one by one on to the flames until there was nothing left of them but a heap of ash.

It was only then that I wondered whether Brian MacDonald had written to Alice and she had kept his letters. You never know, Mam or Dad might have found them and decided not to tell me. Or they might be hidden somewhere in the house and come to light one day in the future.

My baby arrived three weeks early. I was in the cinema with Dorothy, watching *Sweet Rosie O'Grady*, when I felt a sharp pain in my tummy. I tried to ignore it, but minutes later I had a sharper pain.

'Ouch!' I cried.

'Shush,' said several voices all at once.

'Ouch!' I cried even louder after another pain. 'I think the baby's coming.'

'The baby?' said a voice. 'Is she having a baby?'

'She can't have a baby here,' said another voice.

By then, Dorothy had run to alert the manager who called an ambulance. By the time I was carried out, half the audience were more interested in me than in the picture.

Anyway, after a few painful hours, I gave birth to a little girl. I had intended calling her Alice, but perhaps that would be a never-ending reminder to my family of the Alice we had lost. I called her Rosie instead after the character in the film that I never managed to see the end of.

Rosie Taylor was the sweetest baby in the world. I know all mothers think like that, but in my case it happens to be true. She was pretty, had a really lovely nature and hardly ever cried. She was a month old when Ian was allowed five days' leave. He agreed that the baby we had made between us was absolutely perfect.

He hadn't been back in Lincolnshire for long when I realised I was expecting another baby. Our son, Danny, arrived the following April. He yelled his head off when he was born and continued to yell for the next six months. He would lie there, red-faced, fists flying, feet kicking, and scream his head off. Then around about September he calmed down and smiled at everyone. It was as if he'd only just realised that he quite enjoyed being alive.

By now, it was 1944. Early in June, British, American and other forces had landed in France and were fighting their way towards Germany. At last it was possible to imagine the war coming to an end.

It had been thought all the bombing was over, but the people of London were being showered with flying bombs and rockets, killing them in their thousands.

Oh, I did hate war. I hoped and prayed there would never be another, and that my tiny son would never be called upon to fight one day. Sometimes when I looked at my children, my love for them felt almost too heavy for my heart to bear.

Then I would receive a letter from Ian. He would talk about buying our own house when the war was over, of starting his own business, of our future, together with our children. I would realise how lucky I was.

At last, on 8 May of the following year, the war ended. We had a party in Opal Street that went on until midnight. Now that the black-out was no longer needed, the lights in most houses were switched on and the curtains left wide open. The street lamps were lit again for the first time in nearly six years.

We sang and danced, kissed each other and thanked God that we were still alive to see this day. Then we cried for the ones who had not made it, people like my sister, our lovely Alice, who we would miss all our lives.

A few times I wondered what the mood was like in the Locarno ballroom that night. All those young people would be jumping and jiving, having a wonderful time. It made me feel rather old, but I knew I would sooner be here in my own home than there any day.

I wondered what had happened to Sally. We had been best friends for so long, but I hadn't seen her since that day in Gregg's. Not even her family knew where she was. Nobody mentioned a baby.

As I went indoors to see whether my children were still fast asleep, I also wondered about Charlie Kelly. How would it have gone between us, had we met again? In a way I was glad that I would never find out. At that moment, I badly wanted to feel Ian's arms around me. I longed to tell him that I was pretty sure I was having another baby.

Mam and Dad came in. I kissed them and went to bed. Rosie and Danny were asleep. They looked like two little angels.

I sat on the edge of the bed and reached for my diary. There weren't all that many pages left. I filled in what had happened on that last day of the war, then, in big black letters, I wrote

THE END

Quick Reads

Fall in love with reading

Quick Reads are brilliantly written short new books by bestselling authors and celebrities. Whether you're an avid reader who wants a quick fix or haven't picked up a book since school, sit back, relax and let Quick Reads inspire you.

We would like to thank all our funders:

We would also like to thank all our partners in
the Quick Reads project for their help and support:

NIACE • unionlearn • National Book Tokens
The Reading Agency • National Literacy Trust
Welsh Books Council • Welsh Government
The Big Plus Scotland • DELNI • NALA

We want to get the country reading

Quick Reads, World Book Day and World Book Night are initiatives designed to encourage everyone in the UK and Ireland – whatever your age – to read more and discover the joy of books.

Quick Reads launches on **14 February 2012**
Find out how you can get involved at www.**quickreads**.org.uk

World Book Day is on **1 March 2012**
Find out how you can get involved at www.**worldbookday**.com

World Book Night is on **23 April 2012**
Find out how you can get involved at www.**worldbooknight**.org

Quick Reads 📖

Fall in love with reading

Full House

Maeve Binchy

Orion

Sometimes the people you love most
are the hardest to live with.

Dee loves her three children very much, but now they
are all grown up, isn't it time they left home?

But they are very happy at home. It doesn't cost them
anything and surely their parents like having a full
house? Then there is a crisis, and Dee decides things
have to change for the whole family . . . whether they
like it or not.

Other resources

Enjoy this book? Find out about all the others from
www.quickreads.org.uk

Free courses are available for anyone who wants to develop
their skills. You can attend the courses in your local area.
If you'd like to find out more, phone 0800 66 0800.

 Don't get by get on 0800 66 0800

For more information on developing your skills in Scotland
visit www.**thebigplus**.com

Join the Reading Agency's Six Book Challenge at
www.**sixbookchallenge**.org.uk

Publishers Barrington Stoke and New Island
also provide books for new readers.
www.**barringtonstoke**.co.uk • www.**newisland**.ie

The BBC runs an adult basic skills campaign.
See www.**bbc**.co.uk/**skillswise**